DRAGON
WARNING!
Be alert. If you spot a dragon,
keep calm and call the hotline.

Potion
Commotion

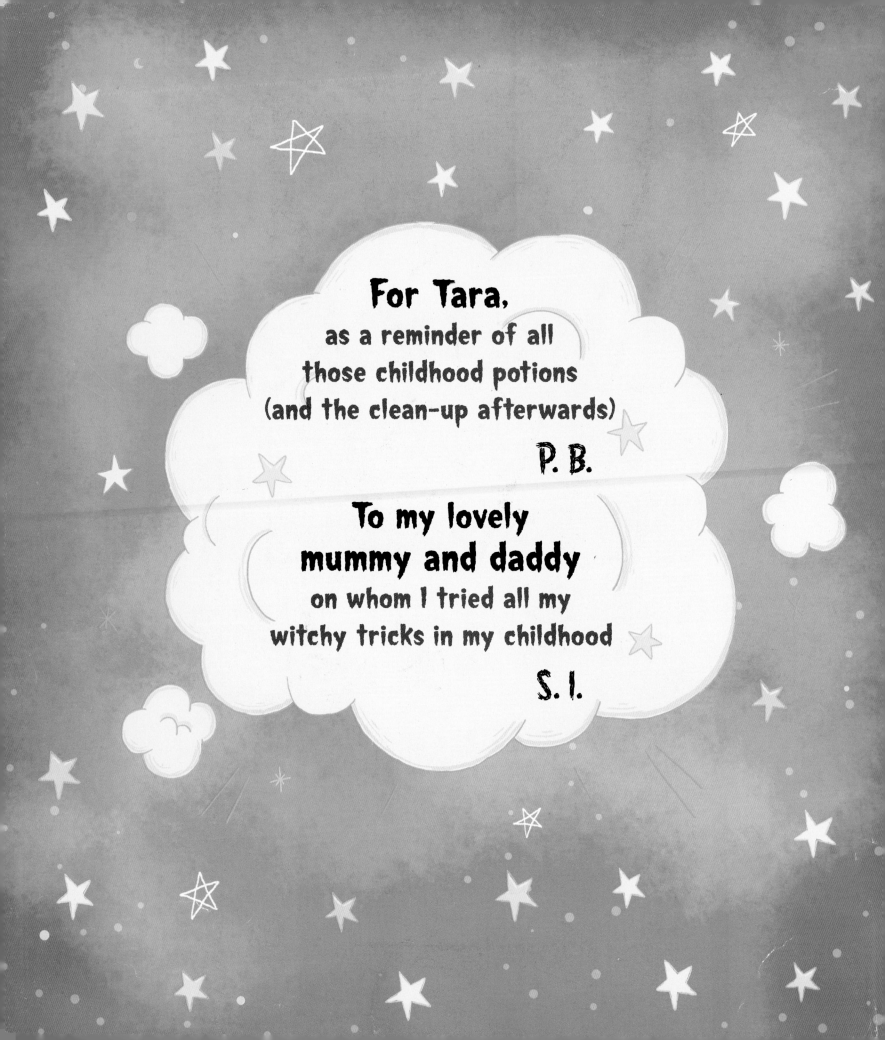

For Tara,
as a reminder of all
those childhood potions
(and the clean-up afterwards)

P. B.

**To my lovely
mummy and daddy**
on whom I tried all my
witchy tricks in my childhood

S. I.

Potion Commotion

Peter Bently • Sernur Isik

SCHOLASTIC

Mum said to Betty, "I'm just popping out.
Please **stay indoors**. There's a **dragon** about.

As soon as I'm back
I shall cook a nice stew."
Then she hopped
on her broomstick...

and – **whoosh!** – off she flew.

"Cooking looks easy,"
said Betty, alone.
"I'll make us a tasty dish
all on my own.

I'll put in the things
that I most like to eat.
Mum will be thrilled!
It'll turn out a **_treat!_**"

So into the cauldron
went strawberry jam,
pizza and *ice cream*
and slices of ham,

French fries and **waffles**
and hot dogs and mustard,
Sugar and flour
and syrup and custard,

Pretzels and **popcorn** and baked beans and oodles
Of Five-Minute-Easy-Cook Savoury Noodles.

Next in the cauldron went **three** kinds of cheese,

And a good shake of pepper (which made Betty **sneeze**).

Two bags of crisps

were the last things to fetch up

In Betty's **mad** mixture,

together with ketchup.

"There!" she declared,
brushing flour off her dress.
"And I've just made the
teensiest weensiest mess.

BEST BEANS
Bewitchingly Tasty!

Now for Mum's cooking spell. How does it go?

Is it **bubble**? Or **babble**?

or... Oh yes, I know!

Hubble bubble, boil and brew
Cook me up my tasty stew!"

The cooking pot started
to simmer and steam.
"Amazing!" said Betty.
"It worked like a dream!"

But something was **odd**.
To Betty's surprise,
The bubbling brew was
beginning to **rise**...

It **boiled** and it **roiled**

and it rose even more —

Then it **poured** from the cauldron all over the floor!

"Yikes!" Betty said as she reached for the mop.

"But Mum's got a spell that'll soon make it stop.

It's Kindly stop cooking!

No... **Stop**, little pot!

Is it Cauldron stop **bubbling?**

Oh dear, I **forgot!**"

The brew had gone **barmy!**
What hullaballoo!
Soon the whole cottage
was filled up with **goo.**

It foamed
and it fizzled,

it frothed
and it flowed

Out of the cottage
and onto the **road!**

Betty yelled, "Eeek!"

as she fled with the cat

Holding on tight

to the brim of her hat.

They **flew** up a tree,

and when they looked down...

...Betty's mad mixture was flooding the **town!**

Then Betty saw Mum
coming back from the shop.
"It's the cauldron!" cried Betty.
"I can't make it **stop!**"

Mum waved her wand
with a swish and a swoop!
And said the **right** spell
at the river of gloop —

"Cauldron no more
boil and bubble
Thank you kindly
for your trouble!"

"Sorry," sighed Betty.
"My cooking went wrong."

And then — a great **dragon** came flying along!

"I'm **hungry!**" it roared
as it perched on the steeple.
"I want something tasty to gobble.
Like **PEOPLE!**"

But Betty said, "Dragon,
you're too far away.
I didn't quite hear you.
What did you say?"

So the dragon flew down to the ground —
and cried, "**Yuck!**
The little witch tricked me!
My paws are all **stuck!**

But that's not a problem.
I'll **eat** myself free!"
It chewed at the gloop —
and then chuckled with glee.

"**Mmm!**" said the dragon.
"This stuff is so **yummy!**
People are much less
delicious and scrummy!"

When that **gloop-eating dragon** had gobbled the lot,
Betty ran back to the house for the pot.

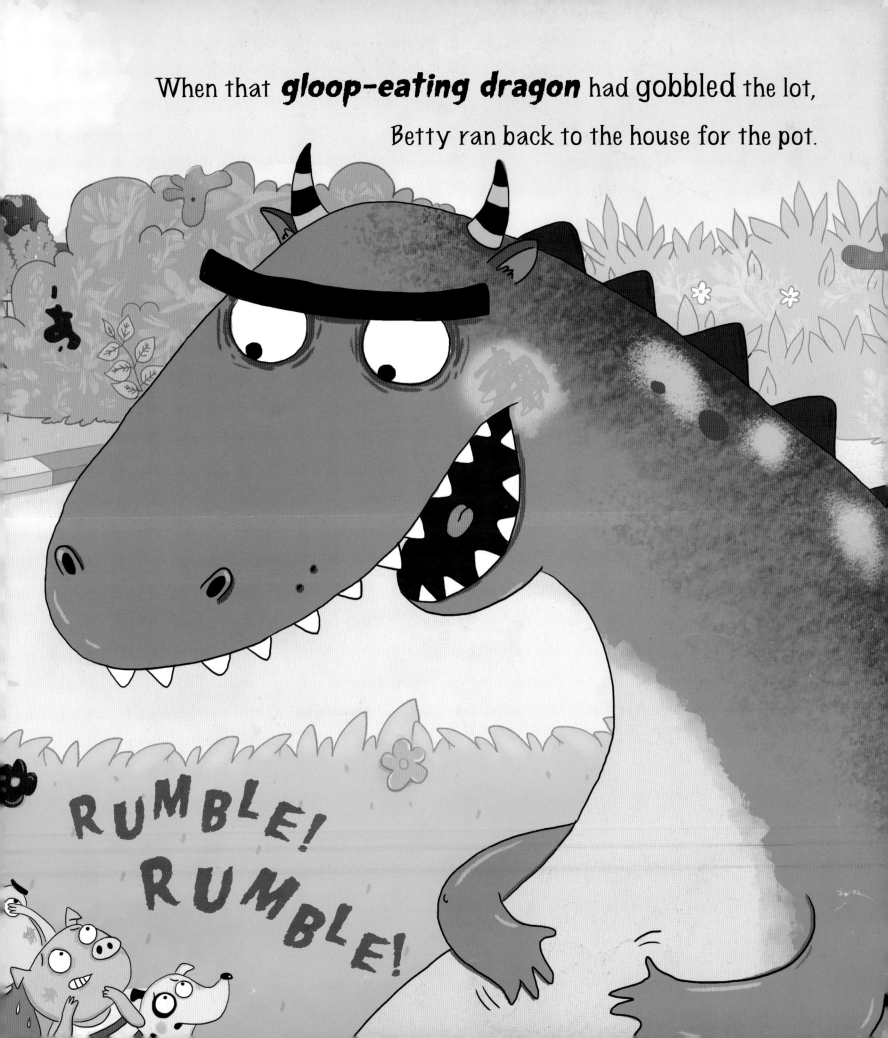

RUMBLE!
RUMBLE!

"Please take the cauldron," said Betty, "and then
You won't **ever** need to eat **people** again!

As long as we teach you the right spell to say
You can eat just as much as you like **every day!**"

"You saved the whole town, **clever** Betty!" smiled Mum. As the **dragon** flew home with a nice full-up tum.

The townsfolk were pleased it had all ended well.

Mum cleared the rest of the mess with a **spell.**

"And now, Betty dearest, I fancy some stew.

I think we should make it **together**, don't you?"

First published in 2016 by Scholastic Children's Books
Euston House, 24 Eversholt Street
London NW1 1DB
a division of Scholastic Ltd
www.scholastic.co.uk
London ~ New York ~ Toronto ~ Sydney ~ Auckland
Mexico City ~ New Delhi ~ Hong Kong

Papers used by Scholastic Children's Books are made
from wood grown in sustainable forests.